Bysta

C000078686

The Bystander Adventure Series will be an ongoing collection of novels geared towards action for readers of all ages. It will also be an anthology of books with the title character or characters changing with every publication.

Over time, the more popular featured characters will be put into an ongoing rotation along with the new novel "tryouts."

Although some concepts will be more geared towards a "younger" audience, all the novels will be considered mainstream reading material and suitable for all fans of the action, adventure, mystery, super-hero and science fiction genres.

The Editors and Publishers

Dedication

To Dan Curtis and everything he gave us.

Bystander Adventure
Series presents:

MK4

Created and Written by

Chris Lambert

In this series of books, this is:

Bystander Adventure Series – Number 17

MK4 - Number1

First Printing December 2023

Cover Art by David Russell

MK4 Banner by David Russell

Interior Art by Rob Sirn

Formatted for print by Sidestreet Services

ISBN: 979-8-3507-2452-3

MK4 – BOOK 1

"Mind Over Matter"

CHAPTER ONE

The two sets of people, one pair male, the other female, trod single file behind one another, through the abandoned mine-shaft. The bald man in front with the lean build and medium height, around fifty years of age, wearing a dirty, tan, military-looking jacket and brandishing the sawed-off shotgun, answered to the name of General Abner Flatline. That wasn't his real name, but he figured since he was forced to retire from the armed services, after so many times engaged defending his country, and being brought back from mortal wounds time after time, he took the name for himself as a joke…and a reminder that not everything in life was easy.

Behind him was a tall, wiry, incredibly strong young woman, maybe twenty-five, with jet-black hair tucked behind her ears, slightly sunken cheeks, but with a startlingly beautiful visage, if only one could see the entire face, covered as it was by thick, protective goggles, which hid a once severe injury to both eyes. She wore a short, leather, bomber jacket, metal-studded belt, shiny, ankle-top army boots that would have made the general envious and shredded jeans that let out generous viewings of black, fish-net stockings. Most would have called her some sort of "Emo," or "Goth Girl," but she called herself, Samson…Carly Samson.

The forty-something person that walked third in line was the man with thick, floppy, brown hair, a brightly-colored vest and a loose bow-tie that hung from his neck. His soft, normal-sized nose separated a pair of determined but kindly eyes, protected by a pair of wire-rim glasses. He was both a medical man and a learned professor of the occult. He was in fact the person who brought the general back from the dead on more than one occasion, while saving Carly's eyesight from the result of an animal attack…an attack that might have been supernatural in origin. People knew him as Dr. Alton Willoughby.

The last person in line down in the mine's many tunnels, was a very pretty, early 30-something woman dressed as if she were heading out to sea in a fashionable peacoat, complete with an expensive scarf around her neck, rather than stalking something evil below the surface of the Earth with the others. Her hair was strawberry blonde and was cut in the fashion of a longer "Twiggy" bob, if anyone still remembered the 60s model/actress. She looked as if she would have been comfortable among royalty. In fact, she was herself indeed royalty…Lady Catherine Winter.

The foursome, brought together under highly unusual events by Dr. Willoughby, had remained a loose-knit group that hunted down and killed creatures and entities of a different sort. That's why their code-name was…MK4, or in plain English, four monster killers!

"How long is it gonna take to track this thing down?" It was the general's harsh voice that resonated throughout the tunnel.

"Or would that be, "things, as in plural, my dear military man." The soft-spoken Dr. Willoughby chose to answer the general's query in a more reserved tone of voice as he wiped his glasses with a soft tissue extracted from his pocket.

"And we do have the traps in place in front of the cave entrance to deter any…things from leaving the premises." Lady Catherine Winter's voice, if that could actually be, was projected at an even more demur tone and volume than the Doctor's.

"Why the hell are you even with the group, Princess? Shouldn't you be back at your castle in England, serving tea and crumpets for some charity ball?" Carly almost spit the venom-laced words at

Lady Winter over her shoulder as she walked.

"You would be surprised in the fashion that Catherine can contribute," interjected Alton Willoughby, the leader of the group, MK4.

Just then, a growling, raspy noise, both feral and evil-sounding, emanated from up ahead, near the entrance to the mine.

"Who knows," began Lady Winter, "All of you may get to see what I can do after all, once my royal spine stiffens."

CHAPTER TWO

Both General Flatline and Carly walked side by side as they stopped at the mouth of the cave and looked out into the mist-covered clearing.

Before any words could be spoken by the pair taking point, Dr. Willoughby offered up a warning from directly behind the weapon carrying couple.

"Visibility is at negligible levels, my friends, so take care."

Within a few more moments, the quartet, known as MK4, left the cave entrance and instantly became enveloped by the misty fog.

Carly pulled her two silver blades from the dual sheaths clipped to either side of her waist, then stopped walking and just stood there, quietly listening to her surroundings. The general also halted his progress and peered in a semi-circle as his head swiveled back and forth, carefully taking in any visual anomalies in the immediate area.

It was then that the mist began to take form, consolidating until there was only the seven-foot-tall figure of a snarling wolf, standing upright. Suddenly another appeared right behind the first. They both growled and stared straight at the quartet emerging from the mouth of the cave.

"Okay, everyone," whispered Dr. Willoughby to his crew. "When I give the word, drop to the ground, face-first and hug the dirt."

The trio standing around the doctor, each gave a confused look to one another, but did exactly as they were instructed.

As the first man-type wolf took a step towards them, Alton Willoughby shouted.

"Now!" The doctor screamed as he dove for the floor of the clearing, pressing a small button on an even smaller device in his pocket as he did.

No sooner did the entire MK4 roster land on their faces, than a 'whooshing' sound emitted from around them and slightly above, but not that slight. As they all looked up, the members spotted silvery-looking balls, connected by thin, silvery wire, wrapping itself around the wolf-thing's neck, almost tearing its head from its torso.

But then, high-tensile, titanium wire, connected to two, heavy, silver ball weights would do that, wouldn't it.

The other wolf creature looked around almost in disbelief, frozen momentarily in a state of confusion, as if not knowing what to do next.

But Carly Samson knew exactly what to do as she jumped up from her prone position and charged forward, leaping as she did.

"Get outta the way, Samson, my gun will take care of that thing!" General Flatline shouted as he rose from the ground and tried to get an angle to shoot at the monstrous wolf, without hitting his partner.

"Forget it army man! Get your own beastie to play with!" Carly screamed back as she landed on the back of the giant wolf's body and began to stab the thing several times in a row with her pair of silver knives.

The action indeed hurt the hairy thing, but not as much as Carly had hoped for. The giant wolf then reached back to claw the young human female, away from it, but Carly reached around with both silver knives and stabbed the hairy beast in the face before leaping to the ground.

The wolf that walked like a man finally screamed and grabbed its own face that had been wracked in pain by the pair of knives. It bent over slightly and then stood up, looking for its prey, blood racing in rivulets from its face.

But before the hairy thing could spot its adversary, Carly had already dived into the thing's chest, driving both knives into its heart and twisting with her wrists as her forward progress was halted.

A long, loud howling emitted from the wolf's now-slackening jaws as it began falling backwards and as it did, Carly cursed it and kicked at the thing with her boots.

As it landed on its back, Carly Samson stood up and wiped her knives on the matted fur of the beast.
The thing looked up at the female warrior with eyes that seemed to question, "Why?"

Carly understood the situation and gave the dying thing its answer.

"You want answers, go ask the 'Animal Protective League,' fur-butt!"

CHAPTER THREE

"Are you alright, Carly?" Dr. Willoughby asked the questioned loudly as he strode towards the female warrior.

"Right enough to turn old 'Spot' into a pile of 'Alpo leftovers.'" She had already turned back towards the group and had almost joined them when a dark shape sprang into the clearing. The shape seemed to hover a moment, two or three feet off of the ground before it solidified and took a solid form in front of the group known as MK4.

It was a vampire, 'man,' if that's what you could call it. It was over six-feet tall, that had taken solid shape in front of them, hissing, with its mouth wide open, showing off its bared fangs.

Already moving, Carly raced towards the fanged creature but her own haste had taken her close enough that the vampire quickly spun on his heels and back-handed Miss Samson across the face, sending her reeling backwards several feet to finally topple over and land on her back in the dirt.

Before it could pay attention to any other thing that was transpiring in the clearing, Dr. Alton Willoughby leapt onto the back of the bloodsucker from the night and clung to his back. But the vampire's strength was so great that it removed Willoughby from his back as easy as removing an overcoat.

But Alton landed on his feet and quickly pulled out a medium-sized, silver cross, which he held in front of the vampire's face. The thing recoiled in horror and then almost froze in position, not knowing what to do, when Dr. Willoughby took advantage of the vampire's seeming confusion and pressed the cross against the face of the night creature.

It shrieked loudly and pulled away, but as it did, covering its face in the same motion, Willoughby pressed the cross against the thing's protective hand. It screamed again. But as the vampire stopped for a moment to look at its own hand, the thing noticed, as did Willoughby, that there was no mark of the cross in burned flesh, either on the creature's hand or face.

The vampire then lashed out and struck the doctor on the side of his torso, propelling the medical man across the clearing. It then turned to face close-up,

General Flatline, who pointed his sawed-off shotgun, directly at the night creature's chest.

A hissing sound emitted from the lips of the undead thing. The hissing turned to words of a sort, an ugly, vile-sounding form of speech.

"Your weapon may hurt a bit, but you cannot harm me with ordinary bullets, only a stake through the heart may hasten my death!" The thing finished with another hiss.

That's when the general pushed the weapon close to the chest of vampire and pulled the trigger, both barrels, and watched a hole appear in the thing's body and stayed there as the undead thing's heart went flying out the back of its torso.

Looking astonished, the vampire spoke in the few moments it had to live.

"That's not supposed to have happened. The boy child said it wouldn't. But how, only a wooden stake can harm me?"

"That's right," answered Flatline. "And what do you think I packed inside the shotgun shell?"

The vampire began to dissolve around the outer edges of his own body, but still concentrated, almost willing his body to remain intact, so as to stay alive long enough to hear his attacker's response.

"Tell me!" The vampire pleaded to hear the puzzling answer from the bald-headed, warrior before him, with the short time left before he disappeared completely.

"I packed it with dozens of tiny, wooden toothpicks, which are nothing more than shrunken, miniature…wooden stakes!"

The face of the vampire went slack, the thing could no longer control the vanishing of its body…and so it just dissolved into…nothingness.

CHAPTER FOUR

"That took care of that, in quick order," stated Abner between pursed lips. "Another dead vampire to my credit."

Dr. Willoughby slowly approached the military man, looking over his spectacles as he did and stopped next to his shoulder.

"And thank God, he lived long enough to give us a clue to what we might do next."

"He's dead, that's all I care about!" General Flatline was gruff and to the point in his assessment of the situation, no doubt it followed along the lines of his history in the armed forces.

Willoughby was about to reply when something stirred in the nearby bushes, where the thicker area of woods began taking hold outside of the cave mouth. The stirring turned into an explosion of motion as some…THING, about eight feet tall, came bursting into the clearing, bowling over both the army officer and the man of degrees.

Carly jumped into the fray just then, brandishing her silver knives, but the thing brushed her aside with a sweep of its harm as the female warrior reached the apex of her leap. She landed several yards away as she hit the ground rolling and quickly came back to her feet.

The thing that seemed to be put together from various lumps of flesh, wires and bits of metal, resembled not so much a human as some kind of 'patchwork man,' or maybe some perverted and distorted Frankenstein monster.

"I believe you've all been touched by this beast, I suppose it's now my turn to 'touch or be touched," if you gather my meaning," stated Lady Winter. She then strode to within ten feet in front of the monster and stopped, standing her ground.

Abner Flatline got to his feet and pointed his weapon at the back of the walking monstrosity.

"Get outta the way, you weak sister! I don't want you hurt when I open up on Mr. Ugly, here." The military man screamed one more warning before he heard a reply.

"Please, do be serious, general."

With that last comment completed, Lady Winter raised her arms, pointing her hands towards the sky above. With that motion completed, a patch of darkness began swirling above the Dame's head. Within a second, the darkness entered her hands and eyes and open mouth. A second later, the royal lady's whole body began to spin and rise from the ground into the air.

Then, Winter began to become almost transparent as she floated in place in front of the monster. Next, a gliding head appeared above the misty body that Lady Catherine had become. At that point, the mist began twirling around the beast on the ground, wrapping itself around it and squeezing, the head that finally appeared, began smiling a grin of horror, with its smeared features and blackened pits that had taken root on the supernatural face as a pair of sunken eyes and a mouth that was a dark red and black gash, that showed more than a hint of jagged teeth.

As the mist squeezed tighter and tighter, the walking monster made a gurgling sound and a muffled bellow of pain. Another twenty seconds of tightening and the monster-in-peril...

...BURST!

Bits of flesh, goo, matter, wire and metal bits were thrown all over the clearing and as the rest of the members of the MK4 righted themselves after the blast, they all saw that Lady Winters had regained her stately, prim, proper and attractive form.

The female member of royalty noticed that there was a pair of lips from the monster that had landed on her shoulder.

Lady Winter looked down on it, pursed her lips and blew, sending the thing that was beginning to talk…to the ground, where she stepped on it, crushing it beneath her dainty heel and well-turned ankle.

"I know what you're thinking, general. And as the great actor, Peter Cushing, a favorite of mine, said in one of my most reassured horror films, 'I can't be a monster, I'm British.'"

She began walking towards Alton when Abner turned to Carly and stated plainly."

"Who knew? I mean, what kind of grit does she have in her to let that kind of crap out?"

Carly replied in just as a matter-of-fact fashion.

"Yeah, I agree, there's a lot of sand in that beach!

CHAPTER FIVE

Still standing almost stock still after witnessing the royal lady make mincemeat out of the re-animated man, Flatline and Samson shook their heads at one another.

"Gather up your senses, both of you," asked Dr. Willoughby politely as he waved an arm to his two team members. "I think we all have learned something tonight."

"Yeah," exclaimed Carly as she followed Alton. "We learned how spittin' weird the princess is."

"No princess, only a Dame of the realm." Lady Catherine Winter purred in response to her rather vulgar comrade-in-arms.

"Now, now, everyone, let's not have a cat fight break out when we have so many more 'interesting' things to fight." Dr. Willoughby wagged a finger at his team as he walked back to the open mouth of the mine.

"So, what HAVE we learned, doctor?" General Flatline questioned plainly as he walked behind the leader of MK4.

Alton stopped and turned to face the three that had halted a few paces behind him and seemed, by the look on their faces, as if they were finally ready to stop arguing among themselves and listen.

"First off, my trusted charges, we were lured here to the mine shaft by a strange phone call. Because of the urgency of the message, we did not stop to investigate, rather we raced to what seemed like 'the scene of an impending crime.' I will place the blame of that on myself, even though I suspected a trap from the start. That was clue number one!"

"You take care of the clues," interrupted Carly, "I'll take care of the killing!"

"Ahh, not so fast my dear," chided the doctor. "Let's not get ahead of ourselves, for without clues, we might not know who, what, when, where or why…to kill." Dr. Willoughby grinned a little as Lady Winter joined him in what seemed like a small chorus of smiles.

"All right, then." The general replied to placate the man of letters. "Give us the clues."

"Clue number two was the fact that all of the monsters seemed to be waiting for us as we exited the cave…quite convenient if you ask me. And let's not forget that they all, when they finally did appear, seemed to appear out of nowhere…transported? I'm not certain."

"Is there more, Alton?" Lady Winter asked politely.

"Yes, Catherine," replied Willoughby. "Clue number three is that the vampire seemed too sure of himself, yes, we rigged the shotgun with wooden slivers, taking him by surprise, but his words, his last words."

"I can't remember what they were, doc, I was too busy protecting us." The general seemed to gloat as he made the statement.

"And a fine job you did of it too, Abner…a fine job." After pausing, Willoughby continued.

"The vampire spoke of… 'the child.'
As if some child, were directing the
hellish trio that we just finished fighting.
And let's not forget that the vampire
feared the cross, but when once applied,
did not seem to be affected by it.
"Possibly a different kind of vampire?"

"So, what next, boss?" Carly Samson
questioned the doctor.

Willoughby stuck his arm into the air,
extending his arm at a 45-degree angle.

"I think we head back to our
headquarters and start the search
anew…this time for a particular child."

"And then we kill him, right?" The
general seemed a little too congenial in
his statement.

"No, Abner, we investigate the
situation first."

"And then we kill him, correct?"

Willoughby shook his head in dismay as he walked away from the clearing and towards the team's hidden van.

Carly made the last verbal comment as she and the rest of the team followed Willoughby.

"You're starting to be no fun, Doc!"

CHAPTER SIX

The team known as MK4, all strode into the front door of Doctor Alton Willoughby's three-story, New England mansion, leaving the spacious Range Rover parked in the front driveway. Each of them took a seat in the front room, while Willoughby again, wiped his glasses clean of any smearing, a constant habit of his.

"Another reason for the mysterious figure on the phone yesterday, to use an electronic voice-scrambler, was to not only hide identity and gender, but also…age. Remember, the vampire did state something about a 'child' to us before he died!" The doctor finished cleaning his glasses and sat down himself on the edge of a nearby sofa, near where

Lady Catherine Winter had perched in such a dainty fashion.

"Well let's just listen to the phone message again," offered Lady Winter. "After all, we did not get much of a chance to think out our plan of attack when we heard the message the first time."

"That, my dear Catherine, is my fault I let the general's agitated state lull me into immediate action, whereas I should have taken a moment or two to plan before I let us all get sucked into the trap that we all knew was going to happen." Dr. Alton Willoughby paced the room as he spoke to the rest of the team.

Carly pushed a button on the nearby phone machine and stated plainly.

"I thought you might want to hear the voice, what there is of it, again to check for clues."

"Dr. Willoughby," began the electronically altered and guttural tones from the playback machine. "I hope that you and your team can come and visit me at the old abandoned mine, near what the local residents call, 'Cedar Falls.'" The voice continued.

"We've met before, you know, and I think you would very much like to have another 'crack' at me, so to speak. There was a pause before continuing. "But I don't think you would recognize me from the last time, so, I am giving you warning! Come to the mine and enter, even though there may be things that are over your head but still beneath your feet. See if you can win this time and capture me…I know that's what you want to do."

The machine stopped and the voice cut itself off. Willoughby began pacing towards the base of the telephone machine and glanced at the return number.

He then pressed a series of buttons on the device and a return number came up. As the other three members of MK4 looked on, Alton continued to press buttons until an address flashed across the digital screen at the bottom of the complicated phone device.

The general, after noticing the address, stated plainly.

"I don't think that's actually too far from here, doctor." The military man instantly began checking the weapons he had attached to his belt.

"Hold on Abner," interjected Alton. "We should probably take precautions with a little investigation first."

"You mean we should 'case the place' first?" The general tried to be demur in his statement but failed miserably since Alton quite quickly knew what was going through the general's head.

Before Alton could chastise or even disagree with the general, Lady Catherine Winter interjected.

"No need to worry about a single thing, general, I've got a quiet idea."

With that she punched in the telephone number in question to see if anyone was at home. As the number began to ring, she placed the phone receiver down on the nearby table and began to become wispy and transparent.

Before she disappeared completely, her translucent form entered the mouthpiece of the phone and laughed before completely vanishing.

"I knew these old 'land line' telephones still had a good use left in them!"

CHAPTER SEVEN

"What just happened," shouted Abner Flatline, the military man of the group known as MK4.

It was now Carly Samson's turn to let loose with an incredulous comment.

"I guess that's ONE way of making a long-distance phone call!"

"No need to worry, crew," stated Dr. Willoughby to the members of his team. "She's used this trick before and no doubt she'll use it again, depending on the case."

"I'm telling you Alton," began Abner to the medical man, "when this case is more or less wrapped up, you are going to HAVE to sit down with us and let us know what this woman is all about!" He paused a moment and thumbed his fist in the direction of Carly before he spoke again.

"And maybe give me the lowdown on THIS one as well." He gave a condescending look at Carly as he continued speaking.

Before the doctor could utter a word, Miss Samson cut in.

"And I would not mind hearing a little bit about the army man, doc. I mean, Flatline can't be his REAL last name!"

Dr. Alton Willoughby smiled a gentle smile and spoke plain and clear to his team mates.

"All in good time, my friends." The smile remained for several moments.

*   *   *

A ringing cell telephone was picked up from its desk cradle miles from the origin point of the call. As it was, the butler-type man that answered the ringing device was overcome by a spewing of fog that sprang forth from the earpiece of the large smart-phone. As the servant fell back away from the desk, the fog seemed to envelope the room.

Lady Catherine Winter, seemed to be, when she became semi-solid, standing in the foyer of a rather large mansion, with stairways jutting off from both ends of the large room. She looked around as if she thought she might find some clues for future use by her friend and teammate, Dr. Willoughby.

But it was just then that she saw dozens of apparitions that seemingly came crawling out from the walls and right in her direction!

She held her breath and began spinning in circles and growing larger all at the same time. The demonic look that sometimes replaced her normally stunning features, now had taken hold across her face, he eyes blazing almost fiery red in their anger!

She became more solid and less wisp as she swatted her arms back and forth across the width of the room, knocking one demon after another, still in the process of becoming solid themselves, across the large and wide room.

But no sooner had she done that, than another ten or so demonic apparitions took hold of her body from both above and below, taking solid form and pulling at her, hoping to tear her asunder.

She let her right hand grow wispy again and lose all form. When it reached the state that she wished for it, she rammed the fog-like appendage down the throat of the nearest thing trying to hold her down.

Lady Winter then held her breath and her arm grew in size and she then flexed her right arm, bursting the creature that she had stuffed, into hundreds of creature parts that flew around the room, taking most of its fellow demons aback, buying the royal member of MK4, precious time.

She flung her still-giant right fist into the head of the one on her left, shattering it into many pieces and parts also. That freed up both of her hands which she then used in a most different fashion.

The regal Catherine, grabbed the demon in front of her and pulled its head within inches of her own face. She then made an angry face that caused her red glowing eyes to burn like a white-hot nova. The demon screamed and disintegrated before her deathly gaze.

But even as she was freeing herself, there were still more and more of the different colored demons clawing and plucking at her!

Catherine turned back towards the phone, hoping to make an easy exit, but was horrified to see the butler simply hang up the phone, cutting her off from the other end of the phone and her teammates! She picked up the heavy oak desk and smashed it down on the butler's head, making him pay the price for his allegiance to this demonic household!

*   *   *

"The line's gone dead!" Alton's clipped and concerned tone of voice and the picture of his furrowed brow across his face told the story in more detail than was needed.

"Hopefully the Princess is not AS dead!" Carly squeezed the hilt on one of her knives, her knuckles white with the pressure she was applying.

"Well, we have the address from the reverse phone number," shouted Abner. "Let's just head over there, ASAP!" He pulled a weapon from his belt with his left hand and headed for the parked Range Rover.

"This is one time that I'm NOT going to blame you or myself for taking off in rapid fashion, Abner...let's get going!"

The trio were all in the team vehicle and travelling within moments!

* * *

As more of the demons grabbed at Lady Winter's body, she soared towards the top of the room to escape their grasp, only to have the wood-framed ceiling come to life and swat her back down to the floor.

As she picked herself up from the floor, she was batted back several yards as her corporeal form felt the pain of the punch from a...giant brick?

It was then that she noticed that a human form had created itself from the nearby stone wall on the other side of the mansion. She threw both solid and wispy, fog-laden punches at the thing but to no avail.

They fought for around ten whole minutes with neither opponent getting the upper-hand, no matter what material it might have consisted of.

Then finally, with her strength waning, Lady Winters slumped back against a nearby wall. That's when she saw it, the thing that made her eyes grow wide and her jaw grow slack. For that's when she saw the form walk into the room as all of the demons backed away from her.

It was the form of a male child!

Catherine was even more shocked when she saw the face of the cherubic-like youth, one that might have come straight from the pages of an old family bible, open its mouth and begin to speak.

That's when Lady Winter realized the person on the other end of the phone had not electronically reconstructed the voice into a guttural croak to hide his identity as he called Dr. Willoughby. Rather, the beautiful child's face opened its mouth wide and let loose with a croaking sound that felt like it had just been released or rented…from the lower bowels of Hell!

CHAPTER EIGHT

The young, male child walked slowly towards Lady Winter as he let the smile grow on his face, a smile that seemed to Catherine, one of victory as the other demons in the room clawed at her and kept her from moving away.

"It's so nice to see you Catherine," spoke the little boy, seemingly no more than 10-12 years old, his dark hair combed straight back to join the longer hair that mingled with the thicker hair on top of his head, which tucked down behind his ears and fell loosely upon the shoulders of his child-sized business suit.

"Although I always enjoy chatting with you, I have to admit that I'm only using you this time to get to Alton

Willoughby." The young demon boy finished talking as he looked around the insides of the room surrounding them.

"And with all of the doors and windows guarded, I don't think he can pull any surprises on us, do you."

Just then, the Land Rover smashed through the front wall, driving itself deep into the living room. Alton Willoughby, at the wheel of the steel-reinforced vehicle, jammed on the brakes and slammed the gear into "PARK."

"Surprise!" General Flatline leapt from the front of the Rover, pumping his shotgun, using every different array of ammunition, both holy and unholy, into the grouping of demons in front of him.

"Leave some for me," shouted Carly Samson as she also leapt into the fray, slicing demon after demon with her magical, silver blades.

Dr. Willoughby then stood straight up from his seated position in the driver's chair in the jeep and pulled out a gun, pointing straight at the figure of the young child.

"Let the boy go, Dayen!" Alton shouted at the young boy, knowing that a familiar demon had possessed the child.

"Why?" Dayen replied in a mocking fashion before holding out his arms and letting loose with a fury of energy that knocked the medical man from the vehicle.

*   *   *

In the ensuing melee, caused by the all-purpose vehicle ramming through the front wall of the building, many of the demons became confused momentarily, giving the members of MK4, a few extra seconds in which to act.

Neither Abner nor Carly, wasted any of those particular markings of time.

General Flatline leapt from the passenger's seat, landing on the floor, and began pumping shells from his shotgun into anything near him that resembled anything unholy…which was almost everything!

Carly Samson also jumped from one of the car's seats, placing her landing in the midst of goblins and unholy creatures which quickly encircled her.

It only made her smile!

Lady Catherine, took the confusion among the demons to wrest herself free from their grips and began flying around the upper levels of the room, slicing a head off here, breaking a goblin into pieces there, and generally disemboweling anything from another realm of existence that got in her way.

Over against the far wall, Willoughby picked himself up from the floor where he had landed after being knocked back by the demon, Dayen. He noticed the other three members of his team already engaged in battle.

He was particularly pleased with how Carly was handling herself, encircled by the many goblins as she was, she just stood her ground, slicing and hacking through one creature after another, sending one after another back to its place of origin, probably Hell.

Alton snapped his attention back to the matter at hand, as he saw the boy's figure float over the jeep, lowering himself down in front of the leader of the monster killers.

The possessed young man spoke.

"Why do you continue this struggle, Alton, you know th---"

The boy with the demon inside choked on his words as Willoughby rammed a silver cross in-between his parted lips.

"I continue the struggle as you know, to eradicate those like yourself, from this Earthly realm!" Dr. Willoughby shouted as he twisted the cross further into the young boy's mouth.

Then the boy's body shook in spasms as Dayen the demon, sprung from the small form and reassembled itself a few feet away. The young child's body then collapsed in a heap of loose flesh, no weight or thickness to it, only a collection of flesh that resembled a balloon with the air let out from it.

"What have you done, Dayen?" Willoughby screamed in incredulousness.

"No worries, doctor, the boy's body is only an artificial vessel I created to hide myself on Earth."

"But how?"

"I created his body, his very flesh, from the…Plasma Pool."

As he finished speaking, Dayen let loose with a blast of energy from his hands, striking Alton and knocking him back a few feet.

"Goodbye, Doctor Willoughby!"

With a wave of his hands, all of the demons and goblins left alive in the room, suddenly flew through an opening that Dayen had just created with a secondary motion with his hands.

Alton took the husk of the boy's body, even though it was merely a plasma-like shell, and laid it gently upon the floor in a dignified manner.

Willoughby murmured softly, in a barely audible level. "Even a husk deserves dignity upon passing."

CHAPTER NINE

Back at the doctor's house, the team known as MK4 sat around drinking beverages and indulging themselves in snacks, food stuff and what have you.

"What now?" questioned Carly, as she used one of her magical silver daggers to hack off the end of a sub sandwich which she took a large bite from. She chewed as she waited for an answer from her team leader, Dr. Alton Willoughby.

Alton answered quickly.

"For right now, this very moment...we wait." He paused as he began to pace back and forth across the basement room, which was his usual habit when he took to deep thought.

But he muttered something barely audible to the team around him.

"Something appears strange though, something odd that does not seem to add up the way it should." He stopped speaking for about a full minute before continuing again.

"It happened during the battle."

"There were a lot of things that seemed both odd and strange, doctor." It was the general that now entered the conversation.

"Yes, Alton," chimed in Lady Catherine Winter, brushing a bit of cucumber sandwich from the corner of her lip. "How could you have differentiated between all of the facts and happenings in the middle of all of that...violence and mayhem?"

"That's the thing," started Alton. "I could...but at the same time, I couldn't!"

"Perhaps," started Lady Winter, "that if you backtrack your thoughts, you might jog your memory to find out exactly where things went awry."

"Yes," agreed Willoughby, "maybe a small touch of mental 'self-evaluation' might be in order right about now."

"But before you start that process," interrupted the general, "I have a few questions."

"Please, be my guest, Abner," stated Alton as he turned to his military-minded friend.

"This, this, Dayen thing, demon, goblin or what have you. He arranged for the trap over the phone, so he must know where you live. I know that this place of yours is almost like a fortress, a very comfortable one mind you, but still a fortress. Yet, what is stopping him from just attacking us…right HERE!"

General Flatline emphasized the last word in his sentence to try and make his point more forceful, almost as if he were trying to get a 'rise' out of Alton. "Nothing really," came the reply from the doctor.

As he finished his sentence, all jaws dropped in a most animated fashion, even Lady Winter forgot her both royal and 'upper-crust' decorum which she always practiced, as she too let her jaw open wide in an amazed state of confusion.

Willoughby continued, hoping to make his team understand exactly what he was getting at as he spoke to his friends around him.

"Please, let us make our way to the other side of the basement, our large, gymnasium-sized work-out room, if you will." He motioned to the team with his upraised hand as he opened the door to the much larger one and walked through it.

"So, you WANT them to attack us?" It was Carly's turn to accent a word for emphasis.

"In a way, both yes and no." Alton's answer was plain and to the point.

"Whatever do you mean, Alton?" Catherine quipped as the doctor finished his sentence.

"You see," began the man of science and the occult, "I have sealed the rest of the house from astral, mystical and physical attack, except for this one room, and I am certain that Dayen and his ilk will sense this weakness and exploit it or at least try to."

"Won't they suspect a trap, Dr. Willoughby?" The military man put forth his question honestly and in a clear voice.

"They may." His answer was curt and to the point.

"Then open a damn door around here and let me bait them." The impatience of Carly was evident as she marched in the direction of the large double doors and waited, tapping her foot when she reached the base of the entranceway.

"Be ready for anything, Carly, I'll be watching your back." Alton smiled in his assurance to protect his young charge.

Upon fingering a button on his remote, the door slid open, both quickly and silently.

Miss Samson raced out onto the large grassy back yard area, only to be amused at the fact that the sun was being obscured by something, fog, darkness…something. And it was only two in the afternoon.

Carly looked around the area and then tilted her head to look at the gathering of ominous clouds before saying to herself aloud.

"It looks like the evil bums got here earlier than expected."

CHAPTER TEN

Upon seeing some movement in the air above her, Carly Samson shouted at the top of her voice.

"Come on, you bunch of creepies, come down and get me!"

But even the young lady who loved nothing more than a fight was astonished as the dark rumbling clouds above, opened up and spewed forth one demonic looking entity after another.

"I guess I shouldn't have opened my mouth!" The young female fighter murmured to herself as she turned and ran back to the still-open basement door.

She dove through the open space, hitting the floor and sliding across it for several yards as dozens of demons flew in after her!

But luckily, the rest of the demon-fighting team was ready for anything that might have transpired.

General Flatline opened fire with his shotgun, which was filled with all sorts of demon killing ammunition and potion-filled bullets.

At the same time, Lady Catherine transformed herself into her alter-ego which was a misty, screaming, death-dealing banshee type force and took to the air. As her figure cut through the air above the gymnasium floor, she spread her newly-formed wings which began cutting all of the goblins and other creatures into pieces.

Shrieks filled the room as the hand-to-hand fighting escalated throughout the gym. It was at that time that Carly pulled herself up and began brandishing her mystical knives upon any goblin, demon or odd creature that happened to be within her deadly reach.

As she lunged from one monster to another, Miss Samson gutted one demon, dis-emboweled another and slit the throat of a third. But in her excitement of extinguishing monsters, she let her guard drop for a moment and let one slip up from behind her.

She was dropped to the ground as a smiling, six-foot tall, ogre straddled her. He stood over her laughing, wielding a small club that he tapped with one hand in a most menacing fashion.

Instantly, Carly took action and caught the thing by surprise. She thrust one of her blades upward into the thing's general groin area...well not exactly the groin, but slightly behind the location of the groin.

The ogre let out with a shrieking howl of pain as he dropped his club and reached back with both hands to grasp the wounded area.

As Carly leapt up from the floor, she tapped the thing on the shoulder and stated these words both simply and plainly.

"Where I planted that knife in you pal, I think you're going to need a plastic donut to sit on next time you take a poop."

She was smiling as she walked away to kill more creatures.

It was at that moment that the demon, Dayen landed in front of Dr. Willoughby. The thing then spread out its arms as if to hug the man of medical/occult and science attributes.

But before it could do so, Alton struck out with a right cross, striking the thing on the jaw, slicing part of its face to shreds. As the astonished Dayen pulled back slightly, rubbing the remnants of his evil visage, Willoughby smiled and looked at the silver-coated brass knuckles that he wore on his right hand, a fight enhancer if there ever was one, coated with raised, silver crosses!

Dayen kicked out, catching Alton in the chest, but only knocking him back a few feet with the lack of force behind the blow.

"Getting weak in your old age, Dayen?" The doctor pulled a small tube-like device from his left-hand vest pocket and fired a projectile into the air. It struck the roof of the gym and stuck there, very close to the metal pipes of the indoor plumbing.

"If you were aiming for me, doctor, you had better practice quite a bit more." Dayen grinned a most horrible jagged-tooth smile as he stated the words that he found to be funny.

The tube-device, now stuck in the ceiling, emitted jets of small flame as the demon spoke. After a few more seconds of time, the flames set off the sprinkling system, the fire-quelching liquid now spraying itself all throughout the gymnasium!

Alton grabbed a nearby plastic poncho from a hook on the wall, while the general zipped up his rain-resistant, armed forces jacket. Lady Catherine took note of the happening and became solid and opened her protective water-resistant parasol, twirling it between her fingers as she did.

"You're going to fight us with water?" Dayen was taken aback with the thought that his forces could be done away with a simple bath.

"Holy Water," replied Alton. "It took four priests over three days to bless this much water."

Everything unholy began screaming as it melted to the floor, creating puddles of evil as it did. Alton pushed a button on the wall and drains began sucking all of the sludge and what was left of all the goblins into a storage-type prison vat to be held until later.

When the room finally quieted down, Alton spoke.

"Looks like we won the day, this time." He smiled slightly as he uttered the words.

"The water didn't bother me in the least," joked the general as he swished water drops from his bald pate.

"And of course, parasols are a must for the royal lady about town." Lady Catherine smiled broadly as she continued twirling her dainty bumbershoot.

"Crap, I just washed my hair!" Carly shouted the words in disgust as everyone looked in her general direction to see that she resembled more of a drowned rat than a very pretty demon fighter.

*   *   *

Hours later, after they had all cleaned themselves up a bit, Alton spoke to the rest of the MK4 team with a slow and deliberate cadence.

"You know," he began, "Dayen was still not himself, very weak, not half as strong as he was when he knocked me out of the jeep the other day." He became silent for a moment before speaking again.

"But what could have occurred between now and then?"

The others began throwing suggestions out to their leader when Alton snapped his fingers in disgust.

"That's it! He's not Dayen! What if after we chased Dayen from the young boy's body that the goblin said he had created from the 'plasma pool,' what if the husk expended the goblin with just enough power to fool us temporarily but was not the real…Dayen?"

"Do you mean Alton, that the real Dayen is…" Lady Catherine Winter was cut off in mid-sentence by Carly.

"The husk, the kid…that is Dayen? Let's go kill him right now!"

"Never mind, Carly," started Dr. Willoughby. "He or it is probably miles away by now. We'll have to create some new plan to track him down."

With their heads down in disgust, knowing that they had all been fooled by the demon, the team dispersed across the room, each to be left with their own thoughts.

*　　　*　　　*

The young boy with the dirtied clothes, kept swatting at the dust and grime that the battle within the house had left on his attire.

"The fools!"

It was all the youngster needed to say as he continued to walk down the road from where the battle had taken place

And the boy smiled an evil grin as he walked.

MK4 - BOOK 2

"Secrets"

CHAPTER ONE

The four members of the monster killing group threw their arms up in disgust as they realized as a group that Dayen still, despite all of their efforts, still lived.

"What now?" The general showed less patience than he normally did as he asked the leader of the team his question.

"We wait and we keep our eyes and ears open for any sign or hint of Dayen creating more havoc." Dr. Alton Willoughby began to circle his padded chair before lowering himself into the comfortable confines of the soft piece of furniture.

While Lady Catherine Winter leaned back against the far wall, Carly Samson paced furiously back and forth across the room, finally halting when her gaze met upon the four framed pictures of themselves, each posing with Willoughby, and one group shot taken more recently.

"Hey doc," started Carly. "I thought you were going to tell us how you came across everyone, what everyone's 'back story' was?"

"You seem the most curious one, Carly," began Willoughby, "but it's up to every single one of you to decide if you want your secrets to be known to the others."

General Flatline nodded in a very imperceptible and nonchalant fashion. "It doesn't bother me at all, I'm just a fighting man, the personal stuff doesn't matter as far as I'm concerned."

"Count me in," stated Carly in an almost boasting fashion. "Just take one look at my peepers and you know my secret."

"But NOT…" finished the doctor, "the circumstances in which you wound up this way!" Alton gave Carly a very stern and long look as if to warn her about, 'getting what you wished for.'

Miss Samson thought a long solemn moment before she nodded in agreement.

"What's good for the goose is good for the gander."

"Then, what about you, my dear?" Willoughby gave a polite inquiry in the direction of the still leaning, English royalty.

"I do suppose it is time to finally air the family linen, wouldn't you agree, Alton?" Lady Catherine loosened the scarf around her neck, but only partially as if not to reveal a dark secret quite yet.

"As you wish, darling." It was the only words the doctor spoke.

The other two, Abner and Carly, shot a puzzled look at one another as they heard the word of familiarity between Winter and Willoughby.

The doctor began to speak again.

"Then, since you brought it up originally a few days ago, why don't we start with you…Miss Samson." The leader of the team pointed his index finger in the direction of the young, fighting lady with the special, dark glasses.

"Well, I did ask for it," stated the pretty, young lady with the vision-enhancing goggles.

"Then, let us begin." The doctor settled deeper into his cushioned chair and began telling the young lady's story.

*   *   *

"You see everyone, Carly was a bit on the rough side back then."

"Like she's not now?" Abner interrupted while Alton held up his hand to keep the general in his place.

"Now, now," commented Alton. "Please let me continue."

Carly stuck out her tongue at the military man. "You'll get your turn soon enough."

"Not too awfully long ago," started Alton once more, "Miss Samson was on a date."

"Wait one minute doc, I didn't think you were going to go all the way back to the very, very start."

"Isn't that the way that we share ALL of our secrets with one another, by sharing everything…right from the start?"

Carly folded her arms over one another, resting them on her chest.

"Go on then," was all the words she said. She turned her face downwards as if to hide her features from the others.

"Miss Samson, whose real last name is NOT Samson was on a date not too awfully long ago as I've already stated."

The general squinted hard at the leader of the group.

"Come, come, Abner, don't be so shocked," chastised Alton in the general's direction. "You yourself know that 'Flatline' is not your REAL name either."

Abner's features calmed themselves as he realized the truth about himself and relaxed in his chair, letting Dr. Willoughby continue.

"Anyway, on the date with this young gentleman, the two of them, that is Carly and her companion, began a walk through the pastoral woods as a way of winding down the evening, so to speak."

"But how did you know all of this was happening, Alton?" Lady Catherine was demure in her vocal approach to her friend.

"Oh, that's right, Catherine, I never brought this up to you before…it's simple, I followed them." Alton gave out with a quick, quirky smile as he answered the question.

"What are you, doc, some kind of 'peeper?'" The general gave a scowl as he spoke.

"Hardly, my good man. But on the other hand, if I wasn't at least a touch on the inquisitive side, none of you would be here with me now."

The general grunted a little in response, not quite understanding what the doctor meant, since he knew that HE was sitting there, even though he had escaped death on more than one occasion with the help of Willoughby.

"No," continued Alton. "I followed for I had already been on the track of Carly's companion. For no sooner had she placed a goodnight kiss upon his cheek than he began to paw and grab her at the same time he began to growl in a guttural voice."

Carly then placed her palm over her face, trying to forget the evening in question.

"But as, what I think was about to become a sexual assault, Carly kicked the young man in a tender place that brings the best of men to their knees."

Miss Samson stomped on the floor of the room in remembrance of that part of the tale.

"But the young man did not stop just then, he continued to twist and turn, his body growing, his clothes rendering. He began to howl just like a dog…or a wolf!"

"What the hell!"

"Yes, it seems that the kiss aroused a transformation in the man, one that had nothing to do with a full moon and he leapt at her, clawing her face and her eyes, blinding her as you can see."

Carly looked up long enough to give a weak grin and tap the side of her special goggles that wrapped around her face and head.

"It is unfortunate that I was but a second too late to come to the aid of Miss Samson before the damage was done to her." It was now Alton's turn to look dismayed as he looked at the young lady who only regained her sight through the auspices of both science and mystical means.

"What did you do, Alton? That was something else that you never mentioned." Lady Catherine gently inquired.

"I killed the thing, with a silver spear, shot through the thing's heart with a modified spear-gun." Willoughby casually went on with his story. "Then I chopped off its head, separated it from the torso and then burned all of the unholy remains."

"You really get down to brass tacks, don't you doc?" Abner gave a smirk of agreement with a nod of his head, almost in admiration.

"Yes, Abner, I do." Alton blinked a couple of hard, long blinks before he went on.

"I saved Carly's eyesight, I gave her certain powerful drugs to keep her from transforming herself into one of those monstrosities, although I do not think she was bitten in the attack…but you can never be sure, you know." Alton rubbed his hand over his face, as if he had suddenly grown tired, and then started up the tale once more.

"The serum I gave her, also gave her added strength, hence, she took the name… 'Samson,' rather than her real last name…Bevan"

"A fake moniker, huh, isn't THAT something!"

"No more fake than YOUR last name, General Flatline!" Willoughby barked at the military man in slight disgust.

He continued.

"Why don't we tell them YOUR story Abner?" Alton squinted hard at the military man with the smug look on his face.

CHAPTER 2

"I don't have much of a story to tell." General Flatline stated outright. "You know how it went, Alton, I found out that there were some of the soldiers at my base that were dying…in strange ways…and I looked into the situation…and that's when I sort of became a monster hunter, or killer if you will."

"But what else happened, or should I tell them?" Willoughby folded his arms across his chest and waited patiently.

"You came to my rescue, doc. Because it seemed like I was getting in over my head. And the two of us certainly made a good team together. I mean we caught up to the unholy scum that had killed some of my men and you made sure that some of my unit, once killed, did not turn into those monstrous 'things' that we did away with."

"But you left out an important part of the story…some important parts of the facts." Willoughby was still grimacing when he made the statement to the general.

"Well, I did die, if that's what you mean, but you brought me back, that's why I picked the new last name of 'Flatline.' I thought it reminded me of all the scrapes you got me out of."

"Actually," hissed Alton, "You died several times, Abner.

"Yeah, but you kept bringing me back from the edge, and I'm mighty grateful for that." The general smiled weakly as if he were trying to get on the nicer side of the doctor.

"No, Abner," started Alton in a very harsh fashion, "I never really saved you from all of those multiple deaths. You actually died just once…and only once. All of those other times you came back, you never did." Willoughby unfolded his arms and leaned towards the military man.

"In fact, you're dead right now!"

The women in the room began to gasp in horror.

"I knew some of this," uttered Lady Catherine in a loud voice, "but not this part of it."

"So, the general is a freakin' zombie?" It was Carly's turn to put voice to her concerns.

The general's lips moved, but no words came out. There was nothing but a silent show of astonishment.

"No," replied the doctor. "He is not a zombie and he is NOT dead, for I put life into him. Every time he THINKS he's died and that I've pulled him back from the edge, it is actually a case of him STILL being dead, but I inject life back into him using my own means and methods.

Abner finally recovered enough to shout out!"

"So, you're God?"

"No," answered the leader of the MK4 group. "And neither do I think I am, nor do I purport to be…Him. It's just that I have many scientific means at my disposal and more than a few occult methods that I use to circumvent…His will."

"Then, why don't you just let me die next time?" The general hissed at Alton, the man he thought he knew.

"I thought it was cute to have a nickname like, 'Flatline.' Why don't you just let me die the way I was born...Abner Bolton, and be done with it?"

"I cannot do that for several reasons," replied Willoughby. "First off, you're a very good leader and quite fearless, something that would help our little fighting unit. Next, you are a good strategist, which is good for the battles we find ourselves in and lastly...I think you're a very nice and kind person at the heart of it and I enjoy your company...although I wish you could get along a little better with Miss Samson, or should I say...Miss Carly Bevan, here."

Carly gave Abner a teasing wrinkle of her nose to see if Abner was watching, which he was, but it did not change the demeanor of his features that much.
"I guess if you really like me around, I guess I cannot complain. After all, I feel alive and it seems pretty nice to be alive, even though it's sort of a FAKE life."

"Oh, as long as I have anything to do with it, you will still experience life…life as we now know it anyway."
Willoughby stood up from the chair and stretched out his arms.

Carly then spoke up.

"Now, what about the Princess, after all, you were calling her 'darling.' What's that all about?', huh doc?"

"Oh, that's just one of the many pet names that I have for my…wife." Alton smiled broadly as he placed his arm around his betrothed.

Abner and Carly's mouths both opened wide for about the fourth time in the last half hour!

Carly almost shouted her reply to everyone in the room!

"How many times does my jaw have to hit the floor before I get the tire jack out from inside my trunk?"

CHAPTER 3

"It all started on my wedding night," began the doctor. "Well, actually on our wedding night, isn't that correct, my dear?"

"Yes, Alton," replied the Lady in question. "Even though it became one of the most horrible nights of my life, as well."

Shaking his head, Willoughby agreed.

"I'll certainly give you that, Catherine."

Alton turned back to the other two members of MK4 and continued speaking.

"We decided to spend our 'honeymoon' in one of her ancestral castles." Alton pointed in the direction of Lady Catherine Winter as he spoke.

"It was one of the castles that she knew very little about. That's why she picked that one. It was to be a new experience, to live in a castle that was hers and find out about its history over the few weeks that we were going to stay there."

The young woman of royalty cut in just then.

"And stupidly, I had heard from relatives, that the manor was haunted, and knowing that Alton already had a reputation as a 'Ghosthunter,' I thought it might be fun to stay up late and experience some 'spooky' things firsthand."

She paused for a moment to regain her composure from the thought of that life-changing evening that she had experienced as a newly-wed.

"How wrong could I have been." She shook her head from side to side as she finished her thoughts aloud to the rest of her team and husband.

"Of course, who would have known, my dearest," stated Alton with the nick-named words of love that he was no longer ashamed of using in front of the rest of the team before him in the room.

"But I still blame myself," continued Willoughby. "Even though it was one of your homes that you did want to visit, I wanted to stay there in the castle due to its reputation…I wanted to see and observe and maybe even capture the ghost or ghosts that were supposed to be inhabiting both the royal structure and the grounds."

Catherine placed her open palm upon her husband's shoulder as if to placate him from his inner turmoil.

Then she spoke.

"But I still think of most of that day as one of the happiest in my life...at least until the demons and the bleeding and shrieking and clawing and screaming began."

Carly broke in just then.

"But at least until all of that terror started doing its rounds on you, the pair of you did at least get to do the happy parts of marriage first, didn't you?" Miss Samson, or as we just found out, Miss Bevan made some childish, yet risqué movements with her hands to pantomime the intimacy acts of the 'wedding night.'

"As delicate as you tried to offset your crude comments about our possible sexual expressions towards one another…no, the wedding was not consummated." Willoughby rubbed his hand over his beard as he tried to ward off any thoughts of embarrassment.

Carly shook her head and softly exclaimed, "Wow, all of the crappy parts of being together like, washing the dishes, straightening the new house and getting attacked by goblins and demons, without any of the 'fun' stuff."

"Watch your language, kid," shouted General Abner Bolton in the direction of the young and seemingly flippant female.

"That's alright," interjected Lady Catherine. "She only speaks the way she knows how to." The lady of royalty paused momentarily before continuing once more.

"With more maturity, who knows, Abner, she may be talking more like yourself."

The young lady of around 25 years of age, quickly held her nose, the nostrils pinched between her forefinger and her thumb in a gesture of revulsion.
It was Alton's turn to step back into the conversation.

"The castle did indeed have ghosts, but they were not the poltergeist variety, no, not at all. These were the 'disembowel' you, 'tear out your throat,' revenge-filledtype of ghosts." Alton wrapped his arm around his wife's shoulder in a slight show of affection, letting her know that even during the telling of her story, that he still loved her even as she had been turned herself, into

one of the kinds of 'horrors' that the
MK4 fight almost every week.
"And this was the kind of ghosts or
monsters that attacked your wife?" It
was General Bolton, no longer calling
himself, 'Flatline,' that asked the
question.

"Yes, it was." Lady Catherine
Winter/Willoughby, answered plainly.

"They turned you into what we saw in
the clearing a few days back, and what
went through the earpiece of the
phone…that wispy, powerful, thing!"
Carly paused, an almost look of pain on
her face for her fellow team member
when she talked again.
"But how?"

Catherine, took the scarf that she had
already begun to loosen from her neck

and pulled the wrap totally from her shoulders.

All around her throat, there was a red, mottled glow about her neck, which seemed to bubble up as if hot lava were ready to begin flowing from the wound.

Both Abner and Carly gasped slightly in reaction to the sight of their fellow member of the MK4.

In answer to the two members reactions, Alton twisted around and spied the movement on his wife's neck.

"Well, it looks like it's time for another one of your shots." Willoughby, the ever-dutiful husband, reached into his pocket and retrieved a needle and a vial of liquid that he himself had prepared and kept always at the ready.

After the injection was made, Catherine breathed a sigh of relief. "Ah,

I thought it was getting close to the time when I needed that." The lady of royalty seemed to beam with the smile she placed upon her face.

"So," began Carly, "she got transformed, but you saved her and at least got her to be able to live with her new condition?"

"Yes, Miss Bevan," replied the doctor. "Just like I've saved all of you, to some degree or another, over the past year or so."

Abner and Carly both shook their heads in agreement before General Bolton spoke up.

"Now, what about your back story, Alton?"

"Yeah," chimed in Miss Bevan. "What's your origin story?"

Dr. Willoughby took his arm away from his wife and walked to the window, where he enjoyed sitting in his favorite chair and peering out the window to think. Before he sat down, he replied over his shoulder to all that was listening.

"That's a story for a different time."

MK4 - BOOK 3

"Willoughby's Christmas Tale"

CHAPTER ONE

Several months after the early summer season faded to fall before transforming itself to winter, Dr. Alton Willoughby, leader of the demon hunting quartet named, MK4, sat in his favorite padded chair, looking out the large window into the snowy grounds that surrounded his mansion.

"Hey, doc," alerted General Abner Bolton (no longer 'Flatline) to his commander. "When do you want to exchange our gifts, tonight or in the morning?"

"Yes, Alton," whispered Lady Catherine Winter to her husband, the doctor. "I think you'll thoroughly enjoy what I got you this year."

"I put about as much thought as I could into your present this year, boss," exclaimed Carly Bevan (no longer Samson) as she waved her right arm into the air as if to get someone's attention. "But you know me, scatterbrained and all…" She left the words hanging as if what she did say was explanation enough.

"Why don't we hold off until morning, people." Willoughby spoke without turning around. "There's still some shopping I'd like to do."

"On Christmas Eve? What's open at this time of night at this time of year?" Bolton held both of his hands in front of him as if to plead his case.

"Oh, there's a place that I know of that's open around the clock and year-round as well." Alton answered in a matter-of-fact speech pattern, as if to hint that everyone should know of the place he was thinking of.

He rose from the chair and put on a coat from the closet, one that shone in a silvery fashion. He then began pulling weapons from a nearby desk drawer and stuffing them into the pockets of his coat.

"In fact, I'm thinking of going shopping right now!" Alton walked past everyone without turning his gaze in any direction but the one that he was headed towards.

"I guess we'd better stay home, if you're shopping for the three of us, darling. We would not want to spoil any surprises for this trio of ours." Catherine smiled in a demure style that bemoaned the powerful and almost bestial creature that she really was, once unleashed.

"The gifts are not actually for the three of you…it's for the world." Willoughby made the statement as casual as if he had asked someone at the dinner table to, 'pass the butter.'

Befuddled, the threesome shook their heads, almost in unison.

"Where are you gonna go shopping, boss… 'Planets-R-Us?' Carly was slightly flippant in her asking.

Alton turned away from a door that the threesome rarely, if ever, saw him use. He then faced the trio and answered politely.

"No, actually, I'm going to…Hell!"

"Please, Alton, don't joke, especially not at this time of year." Catherine spoke demurely, but with a sense of strength in her voice.

"And if you ARE, really going...then I'm coming along also." Abner made the gesture by holding out his always present gun."

"Yeah, but I'll ride shotgun," spewed out Carly, "but somebody has to first give me a shotgun." She became slightly sheepish as she made the plea for the powerful firearm, realizing that she was more of the knife expert.

 "I'll go alone," offered the leader of the group, "unless you'd like to come along, but it is not necessary." Dr. Willoughby paused for a moment and began again. "I suppose I might need the help, but it is up to the three of you to decide."

In unison the trio verbally agreed to follow their friend and leader of the MK4.

"Then follow me, please."
Willoughby opened the door that no one had really seen or paid attention to before and stepped into the compartment on the other side.

The threesome, carrying the weapons that they were most familiar with, stepped in line directly behind the good doctor.

The door slid closed behind them. Alton pressed the button on the wall and the floor began to descend at an extremely rapid rate.

"Prepare yourselves everyone, this concealed elevator will be getting warm, very quickly." Alton made the statement as he grabbed the arm rail that traversed the entire room.

"We really are going to Hell, aren't we?" The general was bewildered as he made the statement.

Willoughby and Lady Catherine said nothing in reply, but as the elevator car came to a stop, the doorway slowly opened with a hiss, leaving Carly, who was leaning back against her part of the inside of the car with wide eyes, to speak.

"Basement floor...lawn mowers, lamp fixtures, ladies' lingerie and...Satan!"

CHAPTER TWO

As the foursome stepped from the elevator car, everything around them they noticed, was reddish-colored and as hot as…well, Hell if anybody had taken the time to look around closely. All of them but Willoughby and Lady Catherine began to cover their mouths and cough violently.

"Oh, I forgot," began the leader of the MK4 group. "Here put these hard plastic bands around your necks, like a strand of stiff jewelry and then press the small stud on the front, it will cause the tube to give off a constant stream of cold air to off-set the heat that surrounds us."

After following the doctor's orders, the general raised a concern.

"I take it, you had already put your tubing on, since you have been here before and know the routine. But why not Lady Winter?"

"You've seen my 'other' half, Abner. You should now that it is indeed hotter inside myself than it is out here.

Even with the heat assuaged by the cold tubing device, just hearing that description from the lips of her Royal partner, made Carly shiver.

"Come along, team, we've got places to go, or places for me to go if you'd like to stay here and wait?"

The other three quickly agreed that they would follow along to help the doctor in case of danger or need.

No sooner did they begin walking through the steam and the craggy floors of Hell, than several demons leapt at them from the ceiling.

Reacting quickly, Carly pulled her two mystic and curved blades from her sides and thrust them into the air above her and in the act, skewered a pair of hellish things that were about to pounce on her.

"Two down and about a million to go!" The young, scrappy girl with the augmented strength shouted into the air as she claimed victory.

Abner began shooting his shotgun that was filled with different types of mystical and holy bullets. In direct response, the demons began dying and falling about him in piles.

Elsewhere, a few yards away, Catherine transformed herself into the flying, wispy, horror that she allowed herself to turn into and began flying around the area, grabbing the demons from close-by and began tearing them in half, going from one bunch of creatures to the next!

Meanwhile, Alton pulled a pistol from his inner vest-pocket and fired ice-bullets made from holy water into the faces of the marauding demons. The intensity of the bullets in such an anti-holy place caused even more damage to the demons than would have been expected, probably due to the foreign aspects of anything holy at the gates of hell.

"Keep heading to your right!" Dr. Willoughby pointed with one finger in the direction that he was advising his team towards as he continued firing his holy water weapon with his other hand.

General Bolton noticed the demons that were trying to outflank them as they were racing as a team in the direction that their leader was pointing.

"Keep following the doc's directions, but tighten up our ranks, the unholy things are looking for a crack in our defenses!" Another blast from his shotgun followed his words as the team continued running.

Lady Catherine's wispy body wrapped around two of the goblins that were trying to attack the team. She then solidified her form, crushing the pair of entities as she did so.

Meanwhile, Carly slashed out with her mystical knives at anything that looked as if might have taken up residence in Hell, on a regular basis. As she continued to carve up the unholy beings, she noticed that the foursome was about to come up against a rock wall, but a rock wall with…a door in it!

Abner spoke quickly.

"I've got a grenade that I brought if you need this door blasted open, doc!"

Suddenly, a smile spread across his face as he turned to his team and spoke softly and calmly, withdrawing an object from his pocket as he did.

"No need, Abner. You see, I've brought a key."

"You have a key to the doorway to Hell?" Carly almost shouted the question in an unbelieving fashion, she was so taken aback.

"Of course, I do," replied Willoughby. He paused before speaking one last time on the subject.

"You see, I've been here before."

CHAPTER THREE

Dr. Willoughby slid the oversized key into the lock space and turned it with both hands, the large, ornate door opening with relative ease. Once inside, Willoughby motioned for the other three to follow behind him in single file.

Within moments, demons from both sides of them closed in on their ranks, slowly stepping closer and yet ever closer.

"Say the word, doc," spoke the general cautiously, wielding his demon-blasting shotgun as he talked.

"There's no need," replied Alton, a wave of his left hand through the air, to signify that he felt there was no danger.

And indeed, the demons held their ground, almost transfixed in place when the leader of the MK4 raised his arm.

"There is no need for panic, general. All of you are quite safe, I assure you!" The voice was so gentle in tone, yet booming, that some of the four began to cover their ears with their hands.

All of the four except Willoughby, looked upward to a throne that stood fifteen feet wide and twenty feet tall. But that was not the astounding aspect of what they saw. It was the being upon the majestic chair that puzzled the trio standing behind Dr. Willoughby.

The being seemed to rise another forty feet into the air from where he sat. And when the threesome finally craned their necks high enough to see the face upon the being, they were all amazed to behold the visage of an extremely handsome, gigantic man.

"Whoa, what a stud! Too bad he's the size of the Rockefeller Building." Carly was astounded over the man's size and good looks.

"Hold your horses and don't get out your dance card yet, my dear child," chided Willoughby to the youngest member of the team. "I think you might have a change of heart momentarily."

"That's right, Carly." The large creature spoke again in high volume.

"You know my name?" Her jaw opened wide yet again.

"I know all of your names. I've met the general before, but only briefly. And Lady Winter…she had the best chance of staying with me after what transpired around her condition. Why if it weren't for Dr. Willoughby here, with his amazing persuasive powers, all three of you might have been wound up here in my domain…with your own quarters, of course."

"Hey, I thought Dr. Willoughby was the only one who knew our beginnings, our origins, if you will!" Carly was ready to fly off the handle in her eagerness to answer the giant man.

"He knows everything I know, Carly." The good doctor stated to the young girl under his breath.

"And, being his wife, I know just as much. I know just how much we all owe my dear husband." Lady Catherine Winter was resolute in her statement to her friend and team member.

Alton turned his back on the giant man and addressed his team straight on, face to face.

"You see, friends, this 'man' was there when each of you had your 'accidents' and was ready to help transport you to this very place…Hell!" Dr. Willoughby's visage became stern and almost granite-like as he spoke.

"Good Lord!" The general could barely get the words out.

"Not me," interjected the tall human-like creature that resembled a man. "You're thinking of the 'other guy.' The giant pointed his finger upwards, out of Hell and towards Heaven.

"Well, then how did we stay out of this place?" Carly was almost pleading as she asked, before she realized that the person she was having a conversation with was…Satan!

"It was the 'barter' system that kept you out of my clutches." The behemoth of a creature answered her politely.

"And I am here yet again to do more 'bartering' with you." Alton had turned back around again to face Satan directly.

"You want to trade with Satan? What for, a dead goat for a dead chicken, let's get outta here, doc!" Carly was almost breathless in her comments.

"What do you want, Willoughby?" Satan looked down from his throne and met the gaze of the doctor's.

"Look into my eyes, I will allow you to read my mind for no more than a few seconds, but I'm guessing that you already know what I want!"

"Yes," replied Satan with a smile, "and they price that you're willing to offer up." He smiled as he saw inside Alton's mind and finished his task.

*   *   *

Instantly, the quartet found themselves back in the living quarters of Dr. Willoughby's large house. Abner and Carly appeared almost together while Lady Catherine came to being, next to her husband, several feet away from the other two.

General Bolton, slightly shaky on his feet, stumbled over to the mantle by the fireplace, where several framed pictures stood there, as if guarding the wall behind them.

"Alton," started the general. "I don't remember these pictures being here in this room before?"

"They weren't, Abner. Satan put them there to remind me of something."

Carly, looking at one picture after another, spoke up.

"Hey doc, these pictures weren't taken that far apart, I know since I was there and each of us is in a different photo with you, all three of us." She paused before beginning again.

"You look a little different in each of these, but I can't put my finger on how or what the difference is."

"He's matured a little since meeting you, Carly, since being with all of us." Willoughby's wife spoke softly and gently, as if she were trying not to sooth the team's feelings, rather, only her husband's.

Alton turned to face the group. He began to remove his glasses and look into the nearby mirror.

Abner thought he saw a dark reflection of age and pain pass across Alton's face, or at least the reflection of the mirror that showed the doctor's face that is.

But then his wife stepped forward, blocking the general's line of sight. She gently placed her palms on either side of her husband's face and recited a certain line of poetry.

"The crow's feet haven't landed yet, they're still in skyward flight.

And when you look into the mirror, your hair's still dark not light."

Lady Catherine removed her hands from her husband's face and he smiled gently, a young man's smile, and in an appreciative manner before replacing his glasses.

A puzzled look came over Abner and Carly's faces.

Alton then walked slowly over to his padded chair that faced the French windows and sat down, peering out through the glass and watched the falling snow.

It was Christmas Eve, and he knew that he did not want anyone to suffer that evening, at least not if he could help it.

"What just happened, doc?" Carly was truly confused.

"Well, let's just say that I don't like anyone to suffer or die around the holidays and I've just assured that they

won't. Not for a day or two…at least."
Willoughby smiled and continued
looking through the glass, watching the
snow and thinking of the safety of the
world.

"What did you use to trade with
Satan, doc?" Carly was beginning to
fume over what she thought might be the
true answer.

"Not much, my dear Carly, don't
bother yourself over it. I only bought
some time for everyone." Willoughby
paused a mere moment before adding in
a weary fashion.

"Or should I say…Satan did."

Willoughby leaned his head back in
his chair and relaxed, especially once he
felt the comforting hand of his wife,
Abner and Carly all come to rest on his
shoulders.

EPILOGUE

The sleek ship from space made its way through the Milky Way Galaxy, specifically to land on the third planet from the sun…the planet named…Earth! The man-like creature that looked as if it had been formed by lumps of different colored, shiny globs of clay thrown together, spoke.

His name was Posit, from the word, composite.

"We're getting closer guys, what do we do when we arrive, Captain?"

The handsome, six-and-a-half foot tall, human man with the long, dark hair and the light streak running through the front of his mane, replied simply.

"We follow through on our mission." Captain Starpath's eyes never diverted from the homing screen and he steered the ship on its flight towards the emerald, green planet.

The sleek, thin, human-looking man that was a metal-gray, white, silvery color and stood seven-foot tall with the power to regenerate energy, spoke aloud.

"We're almost past the planet's moon." It was a comment set in verbal monotone.

"Starpath knows, Amoton." The answer was given by the eight-foot-tall creature that was dark-colored, creature with thick, powerful arms and midriff. The low, rumbling voice sounded as if two giants rubbed stone boulders together. The thing's face looked as if it had been stolen from an old Earth train's cowcatcher and placed over its head. The thing's name was…The Mover!

Starpath turned to Amoton, his second-in-command and gave an order.

"Set the controls for auto-pilot, Amoton, and strap in tightly...all of you!"

The metal-gray man did as he was told and leaned back in his pilot's chair and awaited the ship to follow the computer driven orders.

The rest of the Advance Guards did the same and mentally counted the seconds to themselves until the ship landed itself on the prized planet!

THIS SHORT TALE WILL CONTINUE IN BYSTANDER ADVENTURE SERIES, #20, COMING OUT NEXT YEAR